Tanya White

The Thirty-Year Night

novum pocket

© 2022 novum publishing

ISBN 978-3-903382-69-5
Cover photo: Nexus7 | Dreamstime.com
Cover design, layout & typesetting: novum publishing

www.novum-publishing.co.uk

Climate neutral
Print product
ClimatePartner.com/16547-2201-1002

For my family

Acknowledgements

My thanks to my children and their partners who inspired me to write this, with many long exchanges of thoughts and ideas, and to my long-suffering husband, who has been sounding-board, editor and even typist during its creation.

My thanks to my son Edmund for his inspirational photographs of sunrises, my son Alexander who introduced me to the philosophy of mathematics and my son Charlie who proved the rareness of 'common sense' and to my little grandson Dougie, and all his generation who should not be robbed of a future.

CHAPTER 1

The Last Sunrise

All preparations were ready. Juliette Knightley was bustling around her children, outwardly business-like, efficient and calm. The family dogs, Matilda, a wolfhound, and Barnaby, a corgi, were not fooled, they could sense her fear and anxiety. They played up, pacing, fretting.

Locked in the study, pretending to work, Ralph was drinking again. His way of dealing with things he couldn't control. Freya was only 8 years old but highly intelligent. Fortunately for her she was studious and not at all an outdoor girl. With Philip it was altogether a different matter. Four years older he was entering adolescence with the energy of a time-bomb; always outside whether cold, rainy or anything. His answer to circumstances was just to play harder, forget, deny. Freya knew and accepted her fate, sadly, reluctantly, but she understood.

Victor, the Times reporter, was first at the scene, awaiting the arrival of the crowds. It was 5am, Monday 1st July, 2058. The day the dark screening would go up around the world. A brilliant scientific feat to avert global warming. For 30 years the sun would be screened out. The earth would cool enough by then, and mankind and the living world would survive. This day was to be the last sunrise for 30 years.

'Come on Freya,' shouted Juliette. Philip and Ralph were already waiting. The neighbours filed out; streets were filled. Everywhere you could glimpse the sunrise folk were watching. It was a surreal experience. The atmosphere was heavy with powerful emotion. Freya was relieved that science had found a way to prevent the extinction of life. Philip was terrified of a future in the constant dark. Ralph was already depressed and wondered how he would carry on. Juliette was outwardly stoical, but her stomach was in knots.

Victor led the press. 'A profound moment in history as we watch the stunning spectacle of the Sun slowly appearing, God-like, and rising up to the heavens, knowing as we watch that no-one will see this again for 30 years. The crowd looked terrified. For the next 30 years life as they knew it was over. But there was an acceptance among the majority that there really was no choice. 'And now' continued Victor 'the shield is going up.' There were gasps. A black line appeared across the sky and spread at bewildering speed, sinking to the eastern horizon one way, overtaking and blotting out the rising on its way to the western horizon in the other. A great darkness, which the artificial lighting seemed barely to affect, engulfed the earth. The temperature, which had hardly begun to rise, dropped away again. 'Brilliant scientific engineering,' continued Victor. 'It may seem grim today, but the planet will be saved.'

Some of the crowd gasped and many just withdrew. They would cope. The Governments had worked hard to ensure cutting-edge techniques to grow food and essentials under ultra-violet light. People could continue as before. As the crowd dispersed into the darkness there was no laughter, no fights, no screams. It was as if people were walking into a deep sleep.

CHAPTER 2

The regulations

Felix McGuire from next door called on the Knightleys. 'I've lost my list of guidelines. Have you got a copy?' The Government had insisted that certain protocols should be followed to allow an adaptation to a sunless world. The list was vast, including cognitive behaviour group therapy, various anti-depressants and supplements, Government exercise pods and so forth. Obviously, the gizmos and gadgets and the level of provision in the western world were far superior to that available elsewhere. 'Here's a copy' said Freya, waving a long list.

Felix was a happy soul, the sort who was able to look on the bright side, to make the best of things. He muddled through life, trying to keep his head above water, supporting 5 children: Phoebe, 1, Mary, 4, Michael 6, Anna 8 and Margaret 10, not to mention his wife, Gail. She was a strong woman with a sense of her own importance, she had never worked or wanted any career, and she was emotionally unstable and prone to outbursts. Felix was practised in walking on eggshells. He wondered how the 5 children would cope without the sunshine, knowing that Gail wouldn't. They had not long taken out a huge mortgage to be able to live by the sea. He did it for the kids, who had so loved being out in the sun, kicking the waves, playing in the sand, running through heathers and over sand dunes, fishing for crabs and running around without a care in the world. How on earth would they adapt, he asked himself?

As the days, and then the weeks and months went by, people adapted to a sunless world in their own ways. Some followed the Government's advice. Some relied on stimulants, some stayed stoical, some switched to auto-pilot and just existed. But common to all was fatigue.

Victor had gone to his usual Fleet Street watering hole to collect the seeds of the latest gossip. It had been a good few months since his big scoop on the last sunrise.

Back at the office he spoke to Peggy, the statistical an-alyst at Reuters and always on the ball. 'Redundancies are up.' Victor couldn't see the connection. 'A lot of people haven't been attending therapy nor taken their supplements. Many preferred the juice.' Victor under-stood that.

Jules, the education correspondent, piped up: 'The teach-ers' absences are at a record level. There was concern up above that the kids would wreak havoc, but strangely they've just got withdrawn, sleeping all the time.'

'Haven't the Government drafted the Energy Supplement Regulations to counter this?' Victor asked.

Paula – Human Resources – reckoned that the Government should have done a pre-preparation exercise, get people used to the Regulations before the last sunrise. It was too much to drop on people.

'Ralph, will you stop drinking that bloody whisky. I need you to help me cope, I can't cope alone.' Juliette couldn't handle Philip. He didn't do his homework, played loud music and stayed in his room all the time. Ralph had been in a bad place even before the last sunrise. A self-employed builder, he'd had dwindling work, which had dried up with the planet. He hadn't mentioned the debts, told Juliette he'd saved for a rainy day. He hadn't. Between Gabby, his mistress, and the racetrack the kitty was empty.

'Victor, who's covering the PM's broadcast?' Penelope was the assistant political correspondent, the only one in the office with any sass. 'Brady's off sick, so it's down to you.' This was the break Penelope had spent years waiting for. Her career was her life. She'd turned down a proposal from the love of her life because she didn't have the time.

1st July 2059

'This is your Prime Minister. The first thing I must say to you is that after only a year it is clear that the great plan to save the world is working. Global cooling has begun. I know that this past year has been very hard, but we knew that it would be. We're all in this together and already we can see that it is going to be worth it.

Sadly, however, too many of you have failed to adhere to the voluntary guidelines which the Government laid out, acting on the best advice, to ensure that people would cope with life without sunlight. This is having serious consequences. Schools are being shut, businesses are failing. Mental ill-health has become endemic. Physical ill-health has sky-rocketed and the NHS cannot now cope. It leaves the Government no option but to turn the guidelines to mandatory regulations. Those new regulations will come into force immediately. The Government has enlisted the Army to help to ensure that the Regulations are obeyed. There will be monitoring of what will now be compulsory attendance at the cognitive behaviour therapy groups. Anti-depressant and supplement taking, also now compulsory will be subject to spot checks. Work absences will be scrutinised.

'I have discussed the situation with other world leaders. Some countries have been faring better than others. In some countries an upsurge in religious faith has contributed to greater conformity with the guidelines. In others, sadly, there are serious signs of decline. Many are, like us, making a necessary transition from guidelines to regulations.

There are also material differences contributing to how well different countries are managing. The Western world has pledged billions to help the poorer nations set up better bio-food and distribution centres. So we must all continue to pull together and carry on as best we can. I thank you. Paul Radcliffe, PM.'

Penelope was immediately on the phone to Human Rights Watch, civil liberties lawyers and other people's rights groups. She expected unanimous outrage. A mandate forcing people to have therapy, to take medication and supplements, and do all manner of tasks against their will, with penalties for non-compliance including fines and prison in default of payment, would surely arouse a swathe of protests. Yet she was astonished. The pathetic replies to her enquiries ranged from 'unavailable' on an answering machine to 'we'll consider it later' and 'these are difficult times'. The only angry reaction was from a clerk, Frank, who was very concerned that struggling families could be sent over the edge. She agreed to meet him for coffee.

CHAPTER 3

The Silver Lining

The regulations were in the event widely disobeyed, and the penalties were then vigorously enforced. More prisons were needed to house the thousands of fine defaulters. A letter accepting Ralph's tender to build one arrived in the Knightley's post box.

For the first time in over a year Ralph smiled. 'Thank heavens for the defaulters' he smirked to himself. He'd never have got this tender without the blackout barrier and he laughed inwardly at the thought that for him at least this dark cloud did indeed have a silver lining.

Felix was rowing again with Gail. She refused to administer medicine and supplements to the children or herself. Normally Felix would back down, anything for a quiet life, being on the receiving end of Gail's outbursts was not for the faint-hearted. But this was different. A self-employed picture framer, he knew his clientele. He stood his ground. 'This is costing HMG a fortune to provide, it's been scientifically researched, it's best for us all. If it gets out that we're breaking the rules, I'll lose work.' She glared at him, her aura was like ice, the change was beginning, she was turning into a raging monster, screaming at Felix, 'You bloody worm, you don't care about us, all you want is money, I hate you, you stupid little man...' and at that point she took a swing at him, and caught the corner of his eye. Not for the first time, Felix found himself knocking on the Knightley's door, wounded physically and mentally.

1st July 2060

Penelope spoke with Frank over a cheap coffee in Bonzo's, a depressing café on an even more depressing street, still, at least the graffiti was less noticeable without daylight.

By now they had mustered up a considerable following. People felt life in the darkness was compounded by loss of liberty. The consensus among them was that no free society would force its people to take medicine normally prescribed by doctors for depression. They were sad, miserable even, but that was a normal reaction to their circumstances. Many had found themselves ostracised by bosses and workmates for not doing as others, some even losing their livelihoods. When the fines couldn't be paid, they lost their remaining freedom. Families became divided over the issue. Was the Government's attempt to prevent depression, suicide, infertility by forced medication, proving to be a catalyst for encouraging it? This was the protesters' theme.

Peggy from Reuters gave Penelope the latest statistics for the year. 'Suicide up 30%, bankruptcy up 28% and infertility now affecting 30% of the population...'

'I have a problem Penelope,' Frank whispered. 'It sounds hypocritical and weak, but soon the spot checks are bound to come to us, and what use are we in prison or ostracised?'

Penelope thought. She loved her career, her life, albeit in the dark, the last thing she needed was antidepressants. In fact, she had never been a daytime, outdoorsy sort. She preferred the nightlife, only pressing deadlines dragged her into the light. If found breaking the rules, she'd lose her job, her bosses were quite clear about towing the line 'in the interest of all' 'selfish to stand against it'. They had no issue with reporting different viewpoints, but if they knew she was now a staunch activist and failed to abide by lawful regulations, well, career over. Worse, her flourishing nightlife had prevented much in the way of savings, and somehow, she'd have to pay any fine, and Frank's also – he survived virtually hand to mouth on his low pay. She resolved to embrace frugality, rainy days coming. She assured Frank she'd cover him. They would both watch their step, neither fancied being a prison martyr, that was a step too far.

Juliette was getting ready to join Gail on an anti-regulation rally. She didn't much like Gail, having spent too many evenings consoling and patching up Felix, and was only too aware of the effect this had on Gail's older children. She'd lost count of the times Margaret and Anna had called round seeking comfort from Freya. But this was an overriding concern. She made a special t-shirt embossed with slogans. 'Where the hell are you going, and what the fuck are you wearing?' Ralph shouted on seeing her. When it all sank in, he was horrified. 'We have to talk, Juliette,' he said to her, but she just stormed out.

Felix and Ralph sank a fair few beers together. Ralph was terrified of losing his tender if Juliette got caught protesting. If that happened it would put the family into bankruptcy. Felix's framing business was failing as it was, people were losing interest in décor, it was just not quite the same without daylight. Felix was finding his naturally sunny nature beginning to metamorphosize into a frustrated, sad, man without confidence. The future looked bleak. Circumstances were bad, but Gail was slowly chipping away the man he was. Ralph was just raging, the silver lining he had found was in peril. He really needed to come clean to Juliette. 'You have to talk to her Ralph, at least she listens,' was Felix' advice to him. In reply, Ralph suggested that Felix should leave Gail, but Felix would not. 'Cannot do that, apart from the lack of money, I couldn't risk her having care and control of the kids, no way I will do that to them.' Ralph grunted into his beer. They ordered the fourth round.

Freya confided in Philip: 'There's something wrong with Mum and Dad. How do we fix it?' Philip sighed. The two children, already run down, now worried about their feuding parents. It was taking its toll on them. Margaret and Anna, still children themselves, were tasked with looking after Phoebe, Mary and Michael, while their father had stormed out, wounded by their mother, who herself had rushed out to a protest carrying a large banner. They too were finding the responsibility tough, there was no respite, their rowing parents stalked their waking hours, and the darkness amplified their fear.

CHAPTER 4

The Scientific Breakthrough

Victor was covering the latest press release. The PM was about to announce a new breakthrough. There had been serious concern in Parliament about the appalling statistics. This had led a selection of leading biologists to try to engineer a drug which would tap into the pleasure receptors in the brain, in a way that far exceeded the power of mainstream anti-depressants. Now they had done it. The PM wanted this administered as quickly and as effectively as possible. There were no side effects found in the animal tests, which had been on mice. Full-scale human trials would have taken years, but something urgent had to be done to address the mass apathy, lethargy and depression. It was a balancing act between the unknown but possible risks of the drug and the obvious risks of continuing as they were.

Victor was alarmed, he thought long and hard about how to analyse and comment on this. Several whiskies later, he decided to refer to his superiors. They took a robust view, siding with the Government, something had to be done, and this on balance would save more lives notwithstanding the possible risks as yet unknown.

Victor heard what they said, but something wasn't right. He spoke to Penelope. They agreed a meet in their Fleet

Street watering hole. He'd sound out his colleagues at the same time. The deadline was approaching.

Juliette got back to a note from Ralph. He needed to 'get away' for a few days, 'time to think'. After reassuring Freya and Philip that Dad was on a business trip, she busied herself around the house and then lay down. The protest had been exhausting. When she awoke it was 3am, not that it made much difference under the artificial sun barrier. Something, she knew, was terribly wrong. Ralph had been so withdrawn and taciturn until the tender came in, then he was so excited, then so furious with her in case her protest activity scuppered it. Why was the tender so very important when he knew how she felt about the regulations? They had significant funds in savings, or so he said. Calmly she entered his study, and systematically went through his papers. By 6am she had seen enough, she reached for her cigarettes. She'd quit years ago but had stashed a few 'just in case' and this was definitely a case. Their savings had gone, bills had been unpaid for months, the house was in negative equity. Worse, there were restaurant and hotel bills relating to places she had never been.

Freya burst in, her mother was in a state she had never before witnessed, hair dishevelled, face pale, smudged makeup, tears in her eyes and smelling of stale tobacco. 'I want the truth Mum, I'm not stupid.' Juliette knew that lying to Freya wouldn't wash. With Philip it was easy, but Freya wasn't just academically brilliant, she could read minds. They made some tea, Juliette washed her face and sprayed herself with some cologne, and then they talked. Freya got a watered-down version of the truth. She wasn't fooled. She knew the situation was far worse than Juliette was saying but didn't want to traumatise her poor mother further.

Philip had discovered cannabis. It enhanced his spaced-out state, blurred reality even more, that way he could avoid his terrifying emotions. He was in his zombie mode when Freya related Juliette's watered-down version of the current state of the Knightley household. Freya was surprised at how well he seemed to take it but got the impression he didn't want to talk about it and left, closing his door as requested. He was not so 'out there' that it hadn't registered. The lack of sun affected him greatly, his favourite pleasures had gone, he wanted to spread his wings, feel free and alive, but actually felt nothing, of that he was pleased, knowing as he did that if he allowed his emotions to flow freely he would not cope, they would overwhelm him.

Ralph was with Gabby, his mistress, wishing he'd never come. She was a beautiful, elegant young woman who enjoyed the finer things in life. Ralph was under no illusion that if he was unable to provide life's little gems, then he really ought to consider his position. 'I am so sorry about your appalling financial state and difficulties with Juliette darling, it must be terrible for you. But look, we were never really serious, were we? I would hate it if you left your wife and children, that would be so very wrong … we lived and loved in the moment Ralph, and what precious memories … midnight swims in that gorgeous hotel, remember that Spring weekend in Paris? Oh, and those wonderful nights at the Dorchester ... darling it was perfect, let's not spoil those mad glorious moments with nasty talk about money...' She signalled to the door. A sugar Daddy without the sugar really wasn't her thing. Ralph left, feeling like a middle-aged prat, and started home with his tail between his legs.

'If you went to therapy Gail, maybe you would stop losing it in front of the kids.' Felix was tired of Gail's constant outbursts, now more frequent and more vicious. They hurt him deeply. He recovered, but each time his feelings for Gail were slowly being chipped away. He hoped very much that the new drug, Omega 1 would be out for distribution soon. He'd heard mumblings about this, some leaked memo or suchlike. Carrying on in his current mindset was proving impossible, he couldn't concentrate or settle to anything, and his confidence was shattered. Joy was a distant memory. He remembered his old Mum, used to call him her sunny child because he was always smiling ... if she saw him now...

Victor got a report on his desk from Professor Mankin at Oxford (Penelope had been chasing this). It was his considered view that Omega 1, hadn't been properly tested and its safety was unproven. He emphasised that this drug could become highly dangerous if mixed with certain other drugs or medications, things like recreational drugs. It appeared, in trials in mice, to be compatible with the standard Government-issue anti-depressants and supplements. He stressed that the timescale thus far was too short to enable testing with all known drugs and medications, and advised against use of Omega 1, or at the very least that there be very strong warnings to the effect that risks were involved. He strongly recommended that women should avoid it during pregnancy and breastfeeding.

'I don't like it, Victor,' Penelope complained. Peggy cautioned against it on the basis of her statistics revealing widespread public consumption of all manner of self-medication, both legal and illegal. Victor asked the Professor to clarify what he meant by 'highly dangerous'.

'As I said, I haven't had the time or resources to get my team testing across the board. Reactions will also depend on the state of the individual's immune system and their general state of mental stability. But there is a significant possibility of internal bleeding when mixed with cannabinoid derivatives, and possible psychosis. Renal failure may occur when mixed with chemotherapy drugs for instance. I cannot yet reliably estimate the probability of these adverse reactions, nor can I say what other combinations may be a risk.'

They had heard enough. With full consensus from his colleagues and without telling his bosses, Victor went to press.

The Times. December 1ˢᵗ, 2061

Victor Montgomery, Current Affairs correspondent.

Omega 1 will be introduced to the general population shortly, for voluntary consumption. It is superior to all known serotonin up takers in activating the brain's pleasure responses and is designed to help us continue normal lives in an alien habitat. It assists in reprogramming us from our natural desire to hibernate in prolonged darkness.

However, please consider carefully the strong warnings from Professor Mankin and his team. This drug is highly dangerous if mixed with certain other drugs or medications. The list is incomplete due to time factors and testing continues. There are no health warnings in place regarding Omega 1, although it has only been tested on mice. It is contraindicated for pregnant and breastfeeding women.

CHAPTER 5

The Mixed Message

Professor Gregorian, Dr Randall and Professor Reiss, the team responsible for Omega 1, were summoned by a furious PM.

'What's this all about? Some mad Professor has put the cat among the pigeons. Look I need you to go back to the drawing board, check his findings, liaise with him and his team if you have to, whatever it takes. We need to know where all this is coming from.' Manic research and testing began.

Sir Francis Foulks. the PM's advisor (the bagman to those in the know) picked up the phone to Ian Rand, the press mogul. 'Well Ian, you'd better get off your backside and sit on that bloody reporter, Montgomery, or you can forget that knighthood in the pipeline. Our scientists are reporting back shortly, and mumblings so far suggest Professor Mankin is off kilter, spouts a load of nonsense, is an alarmist.'

Ian's wife Florence had already been to Harrods and brought her outfit for the occasion, their entire social circle had been told the knighthood was in the bag, if Ian didn't get it the social disgrace would destroy his ego and as for Florence, it would annihilate her whole being. Her life revolved around social events and expectations and for her, this would be far more devastating than the shield cutting out the sun. He remembered that night back in March, an important embassy 'do'. Florence was seen wearing the same dress as Emily Rowbotham MP, she was devastated and for weeks wouldn't take calls or leave the house. No, Victor Montgomery wouldn't just be sat on, he'd be eaten and spat out.

It was not long before the unanimous report from the Government's scientists proclaimed Omega 1 safe with most substances, save illegal drugs. Ian, having kicked Victor off the story, got his underlings to release a press report along the lines of the Government stance, headed 'Mankin a Charlatan'.

Events moved quickly. Soon, the whole scientific world was at loggerheads with each other in varying degrees over the safety of Omega 1. Some countries refused to administer the drug, others embraced it. The US and Russia wanted more tests before releasing it for their people. In the UK, its delivery was going smoothly.

Felix was among the desperate queuing up for his family's dose. Frankly, he was having it, risks or no, God knows what he'd do in his current state anyway, the latter was far riskier. Ralph joined him, he'd have taken anything to enable him to face Juliette and eat some very hefty portion of humble pie.

Some two weeks had passed and both Ralph and Felix felt as though a cloud had lifted. They felt empowered, alive, happy, brave in the face of adversity. This euphoria was echoed by many across the nation. Professor Mankin's reputation was in shreds, and Victor was moving further and further out to grass.

Juliette, Philip and Freya had so far refused to embrace any Government medication but couldn't help noticing the positive effects of Omega 1 on their father. Juliette had threatened to divorce him if he took the tender, but he had been so persuasive and reasonable, while really listening to her for once. She was quite moved by his genuine remorse and concern for the welfare of the family as a whole. Even the kids found new respect for him. Freya demanded that she be allowed a dose like all her friends. Philip echoed this. Juliette agreed to have a rethink.

Gail noticed a similar change in Felix. His sunny nature had returned, and she knew that had nothing to do with her behaviour, recognising she had been pretty obstreperous even by her own standards. He was now diffusing rather than firing up her outbursts and had finally taken her advice and got himself a safe, steady accountancy job, something he had previously utterly refused even in his sunny days. The family came first, he had determined, and this impressed her. And she couldn't fail to notice her own children, withdrawn and taciturn, while their friends on Omega 1 were lively, happy, energised and partying, they were, unlike hers, engaging in outdoor pursuits and achieving high grades in class, adapting to artificial light with aplomb. She called Juliette and they agreed to discuss this over lunch at Piccadilos.

CHAPTER 6

The Fallout

July 2063

Juliette was mildly concerned when Freya came home from school withdrawn. She wondered if she'd been wrong not to let them have Omega 1. Concern became alarm when she refused supper. She'd always had a huge appetite, a well-rounded young lady and in the circumstances very healthy and robust both emotionally and physically, who got things off her chest and spoke plainly. Now she wasn't speaking at all.

Juliette knew it was wrong, and if caught, Freya would never speak with her again, but she saw no other option. When Freya was downstairs glued to Netflix, Juliette crept into her bedroom and checked her private social media, not for the first time, she'd discovered Freya's password months ago. She was devastated. Message 1 'you are NOT invited to Trish's year group party, saddo, you will spoil it, you're moody, boring, no fun, your negativity is unwanted thank you'

Message 2 'you are not one of us, and never will be, misery'

They went on and on in that vein, all those kids on Omega1 had an artificial high, they were fit, slim, energised, wild even. But they were not normal, Freya was gaslighted because she was reacting in a normal and natural way.

Juliette heard footsteps, it sounded like Freya. She quickly replaced the phone and came out, duster and polish in hand. She put her arms around Freya, hugged her tightly. Freya broke down, shaking, tears flowing, her friends had destroyed her confidence, torn her heart and crushed her. Oh why, thought Juliette, had she and Gail taken the anti-drug route, luddites, sceptics both.

'Right' cried Juliette, 'Ralph, where have you put the family quota of Omega 1, we're having it, now.' Ralph happily distributed his stash to the whole family. At last, he thought, conjugal rights will be back on the menu, no *en famille* mega sulking, and maybe even some exciting food. He bounced into the study for a quick tipple, this time, not to drown his sorrows but to take the edge off his elated state, or he'd burst with joy.

A devasting report was dropped on Victor's desk. Peggy had compiled the latest statistics on the side effects of Omega 1. No one else seemed bothered, accepting at face value that all was well. Simultaneously, Professor Mankin and like-minded scientists had compiled a revised medical paper on experiments using a control group. The upshot was that internal bleeding, renal failure and stomach ulcers were 60 percent lower in the control group. Life-threatening deformities to new-born babies was 90 percent lower in the control group. The Professor surmised that people had attempted to come off Omega 1 whilst on medications, illegal substances or whilst pregnant, but felt so depressed that any risk was better than suicide, because that was how unstable they had become, coming off Omega 1 was worse than trying to kick heroin, and there was no current assistance in so doing. With some, it took continued use of contraindicated meds, with others, just once was enough. It also proved more severe with mothers in their first trimester. None of these people thought that coming off the drug was anything more than being ultra-cautious, so he determined that that too would have impacted on the results.

As the Knightley family started their first few doses, and Ralph continued his longer-term use, Victor went to press about the new report. Studies in the US and Russia echoed those results, and they continued to withhold the drug from the population. There were worrying whispers from other countries, and denials from others.

The scientific community was becoming divided, with criticisms over too small control groups, non-effective control groups, the presence of too many variables, other results showing contrary results, and other disputes over both methodology and analysis. However, the scientific consensus now favoured greater caution. Professor Mankin was no longer ostracised at medical conferences.

The PM addressed the nation:

'The Government has considered the current medical knowledge with great care. We will, as a result, need to modify Omega 1 before further distribution. A collection point will be set up in each town, please bring your unused supply to that point where officials will take charge of it. We are taking this path as a matter of caution, as we believe in the light of new data, that it is in our people's interest to cease taking Omega 1 in its current form. The Government will be distributing via your GP surgeries a medication called Metaquip. This harmless medication allows the brain to slowly adapt to the loss of the powerful serotonin uplifter known as Omega 1. This will mitigate any depressive states which might otherwise occur when use of Omega 1 is discontinued.

Juliette was so cross, again with Philip. She always had to drag him out of bed. This time, she had dared to hope that Omega 1 would have given him a bit of a jolt, she and Freya were totally energised. Then she heard the PM's address on the radio. She rushed upstairs shouting 'Ralph'. A mother's sixth sense stung her. Philip was lying on his bed, white as the sheets, specks of blood around his mouth. They could feel no pulse. Ralph continued attempts at resuscitation until the ambulance arrived, and Freya waited for them with the front door open. It was clear on arrival, the paramedics lowered their eyes. Philip was dead.

Ralph would never forgive himself. Juliette had been right. Why hadn't he done his own bloody research instead of accepting everything the Government threw out, too busy with his mistress, his drinking, his flutters, he was nothing but a total fraud, he admonished himself. Never would he be the same man again, Ralph died inside with Philip, all that remained was the living carcass of a dead soul. He would ride the motion of life, support Juliette and Freya, would put on a brave face for them, but underneath he was gone.

Juliette became an automaton. If it weren't for Freya, she would certainly have ended things before the pain arrived, her brain couldn't cope with the overwhelming grief yet, so auto drive seemed to work pro tem. Freya faced the reality, she stomached the lot, reactive depression, tears, sorrow, deep, deep sorrow, regrets blame, hate, anger. So many emotions overwhelmed her. She could not function, couldn't eat. It was the beginning of her road down the path of anorexia.

The Coroner found the cause to be the result of combining Omega 1 with cannabis, forming a fairly toxic new substance on a weakened immune system. Despite his age, Philip was found to be deficient in vitamin D and iron. The Coroner echoed the warning from Professor Mankin and the Government's new mandate, and gave heartfelt sympathy to the family, as she had been doing lately, with alarming frequency.

Gail had genuinely believed that it was only Felix who had been taking Omega 1. Margaret and Anna however, had been helping themselves to some of their father's stash for the family. They were determined not be ostracised like poor Freya, and hey, for once they had felt alive. The problem was, they couldn't get hold of Metaquip, because this was distributed in surgeries. They would have to go cold turkey, probably too high a price for the limited fun time they had had.

The Government was prepared for some negative fallout. Coming off any drug had consequences, but the truth was, they were not entirely sure how Metaquip would work, again, they only had tests on mice to guide them. But it was far worse than expected. By July 2065, the position was more severe than with pre-existing Omega1. The birth rate had dropped to lower than pre-Omega 1 figures, and many of those born were afflicted with life threatening deformities. A disproportionate number of deaths were of younger people, leaving devasted parents unable to cope with life and work. Swathes of the population were reliant on state help. These included former professionals and high-ranking managers compounding the financial disaster. Numerous schools and universities were closed due to staff absences. On the plus side, the young were so withdrawn and apathetic they just glued themselves to screens of various kinds, anarchy was not an issue.

Gail was beside herself. 'Margaret, Anna, come here and talk to me. What's happened? Recently you girls were such happy bunnies, making cakes, singing, stealing my clothes and makeup, and now look at you both. When did you last even bother to shower?' Margaret mumbled something about boyfriend issues, just to put her off the scent. Frankly, she wished she hadn't, might have been easier to come clean. Both girls had to listen to an hour's lecture about the pitfalls of men. Didn't help any, that she was so very disappointed that they weren't lesbian. 'Much better off with a woman, understand each other, common sense, get things done ...' Margaret couldn't be bothered to argue the toss, and Anna followed suit.

Anything for a quiet life. It made them all the more depressed, thinking there was an outside chance that due to biology, they might become, in part, like their mother.

'The problem is ultimately, Prime Minister, that we are programmed to hibernate in the dark, so people become inclined to lethargy, becoming unfit, zombified, if you will. That was the thinking behind the first drug/therapy distribution. That is fertile ground for the development of serious depression. Safe anti-depressants often do little but skim the surface of the problem. Omega 1's distribution and then its withdrawal has compounded the problem, amplified it, causing what we see now, a more widespread severe, clinical even, form of depression.' Professor Olav Omar, from the Government's medical advisory team sat down.

'So what the hell do we do now?' The PM clearly understood Olav's point, having himself been long existing on a cocktail of various stimulants that hadn't even been tested on mice, well, at least until he ditched the lot and returned to his own remedies – copious amounts of black coffee, Cuban cigars and Armenian brandy, mixed with exceedingly high levels of adrenalin born of constant critical situations.

There was silence from Professor Omar.

CHAPTER 7

From Apathy to anger

June 2065

Felix had climbed the accountancy ranks, rather by default, there was simply no competition. He thought he was talking to Gail in the next room when he declared 'Oh God, this is so bloody dull ...,' but it was Margaret who overheard. One thing she had acquired was understanding and compassion, having felt so dreadful for so long, yet happily her 'sunny' genes helped her stay out of the darker pit into which so many of her friends had fallen.

'Why don't you leave then, do something you enjoy, we won't starve, there's benefits while you start up.' Felix took a swig of whisky and summoned up the energy to explain:

'That new electric car, the new dishwasher, nice gifts for all of you, Gail's facial, manicures, hairdressers, designer clothes, state of the art screens, bigger house ... all this costs a lot more than basic state subsistence would allow.'

Margaret was surprised by her feelings, she hadn't 'felt' anything since she took Omega 1. 'Dad, we don't and shouldn't need all that stuff. That's well beyond the carbon quota.'

Felix reminded her that the carbon quota ideal was never implemented, only publicised and no one wanted it. 'I don't understand, what was the point of dividing up waste for recycling, itself using energy, and buying as much as possible, more than needed. What was wrong with carbon quotas?'

'Oh, human nature, everyone wants the best and the most, Margaret, shouting now, 'I don't. What about us, if there hadn't been all that greed, if carbon quotas were law, me, my brothers and sisters, our friends, we'd be running in and out of the sea, watching the sun light up the sky and life, instead, we live in hell, and frankly, I don't care what size car or house or whatever, I just want some sunshine in my life, and your lot stole it, no gift will replace that Dad, sorry.'

She regretted shouting at her Dad, she knew it wasn't his 'fault', it was society. She just kept thinking about carbon quotas, it seemed so simple.

Felix and Margaret didn't want dinner.

Margaret facetimed Freya; she knew she had the 'brains' as to why she was talking she wasn't sure, just did. Fortunately, Freya had been welcomed back to her peer group, now that they were all back on the normal low. They enlarged their conversations to include all their peers, including Marcus Steel. He was the school's pride and joy, an IQ of 184, almost put the school top of the league single handed with his eyewatering results and awards, notwithstanding that he spent most of his waking hours, and there were not many, gambling. He could count numbers, but was sufficiently astute not to show it, and used different identities when gambling needs warranted it. He was considered 'cool' because he shared his winnings, was in the top form and was the 'go to' man to mediate disputes. Many a bully was chastened by his sharp tongue. His father had died young in a building accident, leaving his mother to raise him. She received no compensation from the building company, because, although negligent in failing to provide a safe system of work, it had gone bankrupt and proved to be uninsured. She struggled along financially – a concert pianist – and very grateful later for help from Marcus' winnings. She loved him dearly but was only too aware that he was mentally unfulfilled, and often worried that he might one day take the wrong path out of sheer boredom. Marcus had suffered many lectures at his mother's hand on right and wrong, and the okay intervening grey area. They both read voraciously, ploughing through the Greek and Roman philosophers from Aristotle to Socrates and Seneca, sailing through the whole of the Greats from Tolstoy, Dickens, Dostoyevsky, great books by historians and lots of rubbish besides. They were versed in a variety of world religions, and had discussed, questioned, agreed, disagreed, and generally devoured knowledge.

Marcus suggested that his peers should meet face to face in an old warehouse. These meetings became more regular, and as they did so, the usual apathy became less apparent. It had begun with discussions as to why the shield had to go up, what could have been done. The carbon quota issue that had so haunted Margaret was a continuing theme. These meetings carried on for nearly two years, with some dropping out, until discussions and thoughts turned into a plan of action, led by Marcus. The goal was to destabilise and replace the current order and ensure an early lifting of the shield. Government scientific experts were regularly monitoring and reporting on the current cooling status of the planet.

He knew the internet used vast energy resources but would use it for the ultimate good ~~pro tem~~ and then it would go. He devised a plan that would involve a number of people sufficiently specialised to organise certain sections of his scheme, there would have to be an assessment of their allegiance to the cause, that would always involve a risk, but his internet followers appeared sound, and as his Ma always said, 'There are no certainties in life except death and taxes.' The World Wide Web would reach far and wide. He wondered if he was thinking above his head for a moment, then looked at the anger online, all those young people with broken lives and no future, screaming out for some resolve, there were millions. The time was right. He would engage his organisers now. He called his team. It had begun.

While the Government was still worrying about how to counteract mass apathy, technology was simultaneously reaching into the minds of the young with Marcus as a catalyst, turning their sleeping minds to angry ones.

CHAPTER 8

Recruitment and Organisation

Something was stirring in Freya. She was mentally alert and eating properly now. She found Marcus mesmerising, whether it was just respect for his brilliance or lust for his Adonis-style looks, or the real thing, her soul mate, she wasn't yet sure. But she was certainly going to ensnare him. Guiltily, she ordered new outfits, they were at least fair trade and organic, but she needn't need the latest fashion. Feeling naughty, she ordered a new hair and makeup range. How terribly trivial she thought, but Marcus was not going to notice her as she was, there was aesthetic work to be done on her lanky hair and puffy eyes, and her existing wardrobe was just as dull as her skin, so she concluded that needs must.

June 2068

The organisers had been working hard, inspired and keen. Marcus secretly applauded himself for choosing so well. All the activists from small to larger bodies and corporations, both Government and private sectors, including large scientific researchers and analysts, were totally committed to the cause, including those who had fought so hard for carbon quotas and had been met by a myriad of feeble excuses. The organisers themselves were tasked with further recruitment and so the giant snowball was launched from the highest hill, increasing in size and power as it descended.

James had successfully recruited Scotland Yard's finest young computer wizards, all committed to the cause and happily in situ, in various positions from compliance and money diversion, privacy invasion, manoeuvring, to traffic control and personal enquiry.

'Lucy, what's happening in your section?' Marcus enquired 'Specialist engineers and corresponding computer hackers are poised strategically around the country, ready and able on command, to enable, disable, add, modify as and when needed. The cabling and technical infrastructure is in place.' She sat down.

Ibrahim from finances was questioned. 'Whatever you need, got the top brains in banking and 80 percent of the wizards on the stock exchange, a few tentacles reached the world monetary fund. My people can divert, change, delete, add whatever you want, just remember though, as I mentioned earlier, short time frame for all this, we need to move at the latest possible point, can't keep vast sums of money in the 'ether' too long without attracting attention, and remember, not everyone in the industry is a recruit or sympathetic. 'Marcus thanked him and moved on to Louis (bio foods and water). Satisfied that Louis had control of the respective companies from the inside, he moved on to Saskia from medical supplies and paramedics, again satisfied, he spoke with Gregory at distribution: 'I think it must be something of a logistical nightmare, how are you getting on?' Gregory had recruited help on a high level to cope with the nightmare feat. 'As you know, had to have help at the top at the off on my section. But yes, we have ordered locations, calculated quotas and liaised with traffic regarding delivery. It's sorted Marcus.'

Omar from the overseas section explained: 'Obviously limited control here, but we have organised everything we can, we cannot confirm that there were no infiltrators. We've had the best people on it, including Clive Wong, he hacked the Pentagon remember? Well, his men are tops, he actually managed to recruit the Maestro, Gilbert Reddingson, he's the one who actually devised the system and current programme.'

Miranda from immigration and resettlement was anxious, 'Look Marcus, I have had to liaise with bloody traffickers and criminals, because our current laws are so stringent, Governments don't want to openly acknowledge that their lands are either flooded or desert because of our insane consumption. I cannot keep these people housed and fed on the qt without more funding from Ibrahim.' Her request was granted.

Finally, Brockley in admin had successfully secured industrial sized quantities of top specification sunglasses, pens, paper, compasses, torches, maps and wind- up clocks. Courtesy of an organised criminal gang. Rather surprised insurers paid out.

They ended their day with discussions on time scales and administrative matters. Three weeks or so should herald the start of what they agreed to call Operation Sunset.

It took Freya a good two hours to bring Marcus down from a natural high. 'Look Marcus, you cannot maintain this level of alertness, you have hardly slept or eaten much for weeks, you have to take a little time out or you will have a breakdown. There's not much you can do for now. Let's take a few days, how about that little island off Hampshire you told me about?' Marcus remembered his time with his father before his accident. He would take him sailing on the Solent, mooring in a little bay. He remembered the warm sun on his face, the rays forming sparkles on the water, marvelling at the endless sea and the horizon, the sense of freedom and excitement of sailing. Of course, it wouldn't be like that now without the sun, but hey, why not.

Soon they were off, they imagined there was moonlight and they could see the stars. The sea was calm. When they arrived at the tiny island, they moored in an isolated spot and climbed a modest cliff, finally resting in a tiny cove. Freya had enough food to feed an army. 'I promise you Freya, next time we come here, there will be a full moon and stars, the natural order and life flow will be back, wildlife will abound and plants will photosynthesise from the sun.' They embraced and kissed, then both overcome with emotion, made passionate love, forgetting for a while, that they were living under a dark cloud.

Scotland Yard's Commissioner, Theobald Barnsley, was assured that there was no worrying activity of much consequence, just the usual, according to his sources confirmed by the technology department.

Theo was delighted. Meant he could spend more time with his young wife Maureen, 30 years his junior, and their young son Randall, aged 1. It hadn't been long since his acrimonious divorce from Cleo had finally ended. He'd done badly out of the financial settlement but couldn't afford to risk an appeal. His sons Benjamin and Thomas hated him, but worse, they felt he embarrassed them, Maureen being younger than their own girlfriends. It was very awkward when he met them in the canteen, he felt guilt, embarrassment, regret, misunderstood, and all those emotions that can really only be resolved with a good heart to heart. His adult boys were not ready for that yet. Still, he thought, at least he didn't meet them too often at work, they being computer technicians.

There was a knock on his door. It was Cecil Brooks, an older colleague who had worked his way up the hard way, due for retirement soon. He worked the old-fashioned way, hated and mistrusted computers, but he got results and was usually right, always however, delegating his tech side, which he kept to the minimum. The only reason he didn't have Theo's job was because he rubbed too many people up the wrong way, and didn't do 'woke', felt that constantly trying to reword his thoughts was itself 'un-woke' and verging on the ridiculous. This had caused enormous fallout and ended up with him being sent for retraining for a week.

This detracted from his glowing references and results log. He got an interview and was in fact near brilliant, but his 'un-wokeness' scuppered him. He was totally unaware of his faux pas, until he got his feedback. He had committed a grave error, he had referred to a woman as a 'girl'. He never did quite understand what he'd done wrong, but thought if he asked, he be demoted. Having spent his life dedicated to the force, at the expense of his own personal life, he was facing retirement as a lonely man.

'What is it Cecil?' Theo really wanted to get back to Maureen. 'Something wrong Guv, all these computer nerds are saying it's all quiet, nothing doing, but they are all, well, the young ones who are the best and the brightest, at their computers relentlessly. Normally it's tea break, coffee break, lunch, exercise, water filter, anything but work.' Theo interrupted him with a lecture as to why he should not use the word 'nerd' when describing Scotland Yard's finest, warned him it would go on file next time. Cecil took a deep breath and carried on: 'Look, sounds ridiculous, but I spoke to Debs in the canteen. They have just been grabbing a sarnie and water bottle and going back to work without sitting down, no gossip, nothing, not even when the big match was on. Took it further Guv, phoned their other halves, wish to God I hadn't, got an earful about how we've been keeping them away from their families and with no overtime pay.' Cecil cleared his throat, grabbed some water and continued: 'Can't exactly spy on them, because those bloody screens defeat me, but we need to get someone on it boss, someone we can trust, I know something's up, feel it in my water.'

Theo agreed he would find competent technology surveillance. Two weeks later, he hadn't even looked for a candidate for the task.

Freya and Marcus were returning to a hive of activity, ready for action, rested, and determined, each firing up the other. 'I can't understand why they kept grasping for stuff they didn't want, and then piling it in the landfills.' Marcus stretched. 'The biggest joke is that they were not particularly happy, remember the great market in therapy? They needed to be taught that people 'need' nature, that young men need to get back to reality. Can you believe they paid for courses to chop wood?' Freya, agreeing added 'All that mortgage stuff, stuck on a treadmill with no escape, why didn't they realise that no one owns anything in time, it's like a life's lease, we all die, so we only stay there for a finite time, there's no ownership in perpetuity.' Marcus remembered his mother's sadness when her freeholder concreted over all the wild grasses so people could park their ever-increasing numbers of cars, weeks of large lorries emptying industrial loads of concrete. 'It was a great British pastime Freya, destroying wildlife, trees, habitats, but they just couldn't stop, even when they knew it would come back and bite them.' Freya corrected him. 'They knew it would affect us more than them, they didn't care about us, and now they want to maintain that way of life by dramatically altering the free flow of life, don't they understand that everything is dependent and connected, take out the sun and it's not going to work?' Having agitated each other, they nipped their emotions in the bud, changed the subject and calmed down.

'For heaven's sake Cecil, what is it now?' Theo had just had a terrible weekend. Maureen had just maxed out both joint credit cards. He'd already told her that money was tight, between his awful divorce settlement and lawyers' fees, and they had to be careful. The interest on the cards was 30 percent. Maureen insisted she was buying essentials when Theo went through her expenditure item by item. 'Why does Randall need designer baby clothes ... top of the range cot ... why do you have to buy a Burberry raincoat?' As he went on, Maureen was wondering what point there was being with an older man if he couldn't keep her in an appropriate style. Theo was beginning to question why he left Cleo, who always 'cut her cloth'.

Cecil was furious. 'Theo, you have done absolutely nothing about investigating the computer section, something is going down and we may be too late.' Theo had in fact thought Cecil might be on to something, but clean forgot to deal with it, getting too much angst from Maureen. Instead of admitting this, he lied. 'I've got Benjamin and Thomas on the scent.' Clive looked surprised. 'I thought you weren't on speaking terms.' Theo mumbled something about time healing, and Cecil left, highly suspicious.

The PM's office was in a state of utter confusion. Monitoring data on the younger generation showed not only an end to their widespread lethargy, but an actual hive of activity. Older generations remained, on the whole, apathetic, as expected. The foreign office was getting similar mumblings from abroad. There had been 'noises' about odd things happening in the financial markets, and the Home Office was under the impression that there had been a mass migration to the UK but couldn't put a finger on anything substantive, it was just those 'noises' again. Even more odd, why were vast amounts of sunglasses, pens, paper and wind-up clocks being stolen when there was no sun and a flourishing World Wide Web?

Paul Radcliffe decided to engage a task force to consider the ramifications of the data, in other words, spy on the young. He gave carte blanche for the use of phone tapping, surveillance drones, hidden cameras and listening devices, whatever was needed to find out what the hell was going on. Terence Philby was tasked with enlisting a sound team. He soon realised that one of his team was not so sound.

Several civil liberties groups received an anonymous tip off about the Government's clandestine actions. Within 24 hours there was sufficient evidence of this for Victor to go to press:

'Sources close to Government bodies have leaked information to the effect that HMG has set up a task force to monitor young adults by use of intrusive surveillance methods, including illegal phone tapping, silent drones, hidden cameras and the like. The Government is driving over civil liberties.'

The PM, faced with petitions, criticisms of dictatorship style rule, allegations of trashing basic human rights, civil liberty groups filing applications for Judicial Review, lawyers threatening to seek declarations against the Government for breaching the rule of law, decided to back down. This had not been meant to be leaked, someone close was a traitor. And so, a watered-down pursuit was launched instead.

Victor published the latest scientific assessment regarding the current cooling of the planet:

'Top Government scientists are pleased to announce that the planet has now cooled by one third of a degree. This is momentous. Scientists are claiming that it is far too early to predict if the shield can come down earlier than 2098 but are currently expressing cautious optimism. The major concern is for low lying countries and those closest to the equator.'

There was warning however, that complacency had no place and that efforts were still needed to vigorously reduce the carbon footprint from within the shield. In answer to Victor's question about what would happen if the shield were prematurely lifted in the next year or so, Professor Grimley itemised the fallout. 'First, all equatorial and many tropical countries would become deserts. The people would have to migrate somehow or die. Some low-lying countries would flood to such an extent that they would be unable to sustain life, save for aquatic species, although even that was subject to pollution levels. Moving further from the equator, many countries would suffer drought or flooding, depending on their situation, to a less severe degree, but nonetheless the climatic conditions and consequent famine and disease would involve millions of deaths. Temperate countries to the north and south would suffer similarly, but to a lesser degree. Secondly, we have been unable to reduce our carbon footprint to an acceptable level, so it would not take many years for the planet to reheat dangerously. This needs addressing before removal of the shield. Thirdly, from current studies, it appears that human eyesight is rather weak at adapting to any sudden changes in light, after years of feeble artificial light, the retina could be severely damaged on sudden exposure to sunlight. Years of adaptation exercises need to be done; the content of those exercises can be found on HM Government website. Fourthly, the biosphere, the fauna and flora will all take time to adapt.' He continued with what was becoming an exhausting list.

Freya and Marcus were expecting such a report, but hearing the evidence so boldly thrust at them, with no apparent wiggle-room, left them both aghast. 'Freya, we could be the cause, if we go ahead with Sunset, of millions of deaths. I know, we had distribution centres, we can deliver shades, food, medications, and yes, we can reduce the footprint overnight, I know this mitigates the scientists' prognosis, but still, there will be too many casualties if we go down this road.' He put his head in his hands, he was distraught. 'Look Marcus, you know what will happen if we don't. Lifestyles won't change, that's why we are in this mess, it will happen again, even the scientists are worried about that, no one was interested in carbon quotas then and they are certainly not now. So there are going to be billions of lives lost if we do nothing. Unless we have civil war, or world war, but that's looking at unpalatable numbers of deaths too.' She looked at Marcus, totally disorientated, his inner pain and anguish was expressing itself physically. At that moment he did not appear to her as the strong leader she had considered him to be, and she found this disturbing. 'Marcus, one way or another, you'd better make up your mind. We have thousands of people putting everything they have at risk, waiting in precarious positions, knowing they could be arrested any minute, just waiting for the green light. They are entitled to know if it's on or off, they cannot be expected to put themselves in danger whilst you prevaricate. Take four hours Marcus, go walkabout, work out your position, and come back by 7pm with a decision, and I will help you enact it.'

Marcus wasn't religious, his God was nature. Yet he found himself in a London Buddhist Temple. He used to laugh inwardly at people who meditated, and here he was, doing just that. He had to empty his mind and get control of it, before forming his decision. He walked from the Temple, pacing the streets in the artificial gloom. He remembered the days when he'd watch the night stars picking out the Great Bear, Orion, Polaris, Cassiopeia, Leo the moon's hypnotic, wondrous light revealing enchanting shadows and silhouettes over the earth. He remembered the clouds casting formations to fire the imagination, and the sun, it's wonder, how it reached out its magical rays engulfing and warming the earth and lighting the natural world, and the very soul of every being, giving energy and life to all it passed. How much better, fresher the food used to be, he remembered some article about how engineered food was far less nutritious. He remembered how people used to be, singing, dancing, fighting, yes, but most embraced the joie de vivre. Now it was unprecedented suicide rates, serious depression across the nations, apathy, negativity, it was no life trying to outsmart the natural world. Even his love for Freya was tainted with dark thoughts.

He turned towards home and as he turned to the flip side of the argument, he was deep in thought. He found he could in fact think very clearly: 'might be something in that mindfulness lark,' he smiled to himself. What right had he to press on people his idea of what should be. Those on board Operation Sunset were willing parties, true, but what about the millions of other people they were going to just usher around to distribution centres and treat like sheep. He was not democratically elected, not that he thought that made a lot of difference, looking at some of the leaders around him, but that wasn't the point. These people had not been consulted, for obvious reasons, the whole thing wouldn't be plausible, they would have stopped it, still might. He questioned his utter arrogance, what had he been thinking? Years of planning, work, effort, strain, all for nothing. Worse, he thought was all those poor sods seduced by his charisma diligently carrying out his mandate. They'd all broken the law big time, probably still be in jail when the shield was legally lifted, and it was his fault. He hastened his step. No more brooding, there was much to be done, he had to dismantle the entire revolution, a tall order, compounded by the reaction he would receive from his dedicated followers, all keen and ready, awaiting a green light, he wasn't sure how they would react to a red one.

Freya had been doing some pacing too. She was getting concerned that Marcus was losing his nerve. For hours she had been making excuses to their organisers on his behalf. Miranda from immigration was particularly worried. 'Look Freya, I need a time, I've got thousands of illegal settlers in hiding, our sources reckon the Home Office have their feelers out, God knows any time they could be arrested and stuck in that disgusting centre, you know, those prefabs with barbed wire fencing. They'd all perish with no high-tech shades, food supplies, access to medicine, they would be locked up, then the chaos, they may not make it to the distribution centres, it's not like the prisons where you have 'inside' people Freya, and they are already run down.'

Freya assured her that Marcus was busy finalising the details and would revert to her shortly. But then Omar called. 'Got to speak with Marcus, I have one thousand hackers under me in overseas section getting twitchy, if they get sussed, it won't be a nice trial with lawyers, some will end up as eunuchs.' He did not buy into Freya's excuse for Marcus not being online. 'What the fuck is going on? I cannot keep all these people on high alert indefinitely, the cracks are beginning to show.'

Marcus walked in. 'Give me one hour,' she begged. Omar was rattled and slightly cracking himself, but he conceded the hour.

CHAPTER 9

Anxiety

Cecil went over Theo's head right to the top. By sheer determination and fearmongering, he found a path to the PM. He was welcomed in politely by the PM's private secretary who sat down with them. 'Prime Minister' began Cecil: 'Something disastrous is brewing that will make the shield look uneventful. I've had surveillance on a phenomenal scale, ruined the Met's financial budget for the year, but it was worth it. I will admit now, some of the surveillance wasn't legal, but frankly worrying about whether it will stand up in court will be irrelevant, because it looks like there won't be any courts. I have these records for you.' He placed a bundle of paperwork before the PM, didn't trust putting anything on computer unless there was no choice. 'They show that there have been major discrepancies across the board, large sums of money disappearing into the ether, Immigration figures going AWOL, traffic screaming about computer hackers, disappearing supplies, unprecedented energy use from the World Wide Web, and mumblings from our overseas contacts about odd exchanges from people here, but they cannot understand them. Someone mentioned something called "Operation Sunset".'

The PM buried his nose in the paperwork for some time, muttering occasionally to his private secretary, while

Cecil sat ignored, twiddling his thumbs. 'Why wasn't this brought to my attention earlier, this could be a time bomb and we don't know the bloody times?' The PM looked angrily at Cecil, who felt incensed. He'd been badgering Theo about this for months and only accessed the PM by stealth. He was damned if he was going to take the fall and reverted to his normal mode. 'If any one higher up the bloody pole had listened to me in the first place instead of faffing about, and Government departments hadn't kept returning my memos and applications because I hadn't asked nicely or used the wrong words, if I had been taken seriously instead of treated like old fart who didn't know his 'girl' from his 'woman', or his hacker from his nerd, or his demand from his please ...' The private secretary interrupted: 'Thank you, that will be all.' Cecil left, wounded, but relieved someone with clout was actually on the ball.

The PM looked solemn. He turned to his private secretary: 'This is between you and me, and others on a need-to-know basis only. I want you to track down Cuthbert Rawlinson as soon as possible.' The private secretary looked aghast. 'But Prime Minister, he's a disgraced ex MP, disbarred by the Bar Council, he was actually found guilty of numerous irregularities by the Tribunal, and although the CPS could only charge him with attempting to pervert the course of justice in a small case, everyone knows about his contacts with the underworld and associations with certain mercenaries. Just couldn't nail him for the big fry, too rich and powerful. The old commissioner reckoned he dabbled for fun, didn't need the money with all his assets.'

'Oh, for heaven's sake!' The PM was rattled now, and this was expressed in anger. 'You are being totally paranoid, a man is not guilty until so proven, and he wasn't even charged with the serious offences. I know his career was in tatters and he's been put out to grass, but I want him back. He's the only one who has feelers in every known political pie. What else can I do, I've tried the legal route, ok, grey-coloured legal route, and had civil libertarians throw it in my face. Now the situation has escalated and I have no choice but to go down the red route.' The private secretary understood but felt very queasy about it all.

Cuthbert had been born into an enormous amount of new money. His father, Bruce, had turned a corner shop into a multinational food and clothing chain. His mother, Jean, was on the board of her family's numerous machinery factories, again, built up by her grandfather from precious little. At some stage, Bruce had changed his surname from Nags to Rawlinson. He later collected an MBE for his services to manufacturing, as Jean had done earlier.

Cuthbert was their only child. Financially he lacked absolutely nothing, sent to the best schools, lavish holidays and so forth. But there was a dark side to Bruce. He lacked empathy, was incredibly narcissistic, but worst of all, he ruled the household like a man of steel. He had angry, violent outbursts, when Cuthbert and his mum would hide. He'd source compromising information on immediate employees who were privy to his behaviours and blackmail them into secrecy. This was compounded by his well-honed ability to manipulate. Yet, to the outside world he was charming, fun, a good sport, and clearly able to mimic empathy if required. Jean, once a confident, bright, witty young lady, had through the years become totally cold and empty inside, but for Cuthbert's sake, she kept up appearances. She was often spotted in Harrods sporting designer shades in midnight blue, and it wasn't a style statement. Bruce had managed to alienate her old friends, preferring her to socialise with the rather fickle 'in crowd'. She was to all extent and purposes a broken woman and couldn't really help Cuthbert in any meaningful way.

As a child, Cuthbert learned to bury his feelings, and by the time he reached adulthood, there were no emotions to bury. Though he wanted to travel the world, he read for the Bar. Bruce insisted that his 'empire' needed a sound commercial lawyer. It was there that Cuthbert began socialising with some of his less savoury clients who introduced him to a whole new world. Soon he was immersed in shady dealings that yielded considerable profits, a clandestine business from little men to mercenaries. Bruce knew and, totally unofficially, approved.

None of the Rawlinsons really cared much about living under the shield, they never really enjoyed the great outdoors, well, Jean did to be fair, but only when younger. They lacked any sense of awe and wonder and were not happy.

Cuthbert was with one of his paid companions when he got the call from Mia at MI5. 'The PM wants to see you asap. We'll send a car round in 15 minutes. Cuthbert downed a double whisky and felt as alive as he could be. It pampered his ego, he could smell power, control, excitement. The cause was totally irrelevant to him.

CHAPTER 10

No Going Back

Freya read Marcus' face. She knew he wanted to pull everyone out. The problem was, she didn't. Remembering Philip's death and the subsequent destruction of her parents, who barely functioned now, and thinking about all those people with their lives sucked from them by this vast, foreboding, unnatural shield looking down with gloom, she was determined to act.

Patiently she listened to Marcus, fully aware he would not change his mind. Her very soul quivered at the thought that what she was about to do would have the effect of destroying their love forever.

Freya fetched Marcus a long cool drink, having added 'niton' a strong fast acting sedative. 'You rest a while, take 10 minutes, while I fire up the equipment ready to notify the organisers that we are aborting the operation'.

'Thank you, my darling, you are my soulmate. I love you so much' and he fell into a deep sleep.

Freya tapped in Marcus' secure code and gave the organisers the green light.

Traffic, rail and bus networks were the first to go, causing unprecedented travel chaos. Cuthbert was in the middle of it being driven by Graham, the MI5 driver. Cuthbert was not good with disorder, and felt his blood pressure rising, his body tensing, and then, the resulting angry outburst. 'Fuck it you idiot, drive through the bloody lights, they are obviously out.' He picked the wrong man. Graham may not have had money and power, but his job often involved him putting his life on the line for pitiful remuneration. He was not letting this awful creature treat him like garbage. Graham stopped the car. 'I am not the architect of this chaos, but I am the service's most highly skilled driver, if I could dodge through without actually killing us I would, so shut up or put up.'

Cuthbert overreacted, Graham had pushed the wrong button, hidden impulse memories evoked raging alarm bells, a catalyst for turning anger into violent action. He grabbed Graham around the neck and pulled tightly until he could barely breathe, then swung out, opened the driver's door, pulled Graham out and flung him on the road, leaving him to crawl onto the kerb, narrowly missing being run over by oncoming cars.

Cuthbert took over the wheel and drove like a maniac, angry at life, at his father, at humanity, at everything, zigzagging around other cars, racing dead lights, cursing the fact he'd had two large whiskies, they slowed his normally razor-sharp reactions. Another lunatic was racing around the opposite bend. It was a very ugly scene. All nearby traffic stopped. People wrapped them in warm clothing from their own backs, ambulances were called, but they all knew it would be futile in the chaos. Both drivers died within 20 minutes of one another.

Accidents were abundant, there was carnage on the roads, the artificial lighting was out, along with the signals. Cries of help were left unanswered; people were in shock. Simultaneously, Government security, the financial institutions, all emergency services and basic infrastructure ceased working. The World Wide Web and the computerised world was dead. The shield began to dismantle, torn from its complex technological trunk.

Ralph nearly choked on his tipple. 'What the hell ...' he cried out to Juliette, who was shaken out of her automaton state. 'Where's Freya?' she shouted back. She suddenly realised that since Philip's death, she had totally side-tracked Freya, she had been a shocking mother she chastised herself. She did remember Freya mumbling about leaving for a while, boyfriend, work, she hadn't been listening. She grabbed a torch which she shared with Ralph (she was very glad she hadn't thrown it out with her decluttering phase which she had thought would calm her mind – it didn't, half the clutter had to be replaced). Instinctively they went to her bedroom, and there it was, the proverbial envelope addressed to mum and dad, not exactly hidden but tucked away in a drawer with teddy Blythe. They reread the letter several times, trying to work out if it was fact or fiction:

'Hi Mum, Dad, under my bed there is a box of essentials you will need to survive on for a while. Soon, every location will have its own makeshift distribution centre, everything has been organised. You will shortly see people making their way to such centres. Remember to wear the shades in the box. We will meet again, I am sure. You both know that humanity couldn't survive much more, something had to be done, love from Freya.'

They would have dismissed the letter as fiction, had it not been for the blackout and the neighbours running around outside. As Ralph and Juliette held one another, trying to gain strength, Margaret and Anna were bringing Felix and Gail up to speed and conceding their roles in the affair. Gail glared at Felix. 'It's your bloody fault, you were such a useless father, that's why we have these awful idiot daughters, you never let me scold them, all this bloody 'woke this woke that', when what they needed was a bloody good hiding, well they are getting one now.' The girls cowered as she tensed up and rushed towards them. Felix grabbed her first and slapped her around the face. She stood, stunned but not as surprised as Felix, this was utterly against his nature, he'd never struck anyone or anything in his life, let alone a woman. All the children, Phoebe, Mary, Michael, Anna and Margaret snuggled up to their father. 'Thank you for protecting us daddy,' sobbed Anna. This was the first time in her married life that Gail had some insight into her own toxic nature, and she didn't like what she saw.

Marcus awoke to an earth-defying bang as the shield disintegrated violently. Had humanity met its match? People were shocked, terrified, some running, others screaming, some just stood there, as though waiting for it all to stop, knowing it wouldn't, others resigned themselves to Armageddon, a few prayed. Samaritans tried to help by scooping up lost children and consoling as best they can. A little girl was lying in the road clutching a doll. A passer-by picked her up, 'My mummy, my mummy, she's under that car, can you get her...' the Samaritan looked, her mother was in several pieces. She held the little girl tightly wondering what on earth to do, when another bang disorientated them both, and they fell to the ground in shock. The emergency services were impotent, and the PM's office couldn't even contact the army.

In Whitehall, the generators were up, but that was it. They couldn't use their vehicles to get to the Government secure location because of the outside blockage and mayhem. The PM took his main people and started to walk, they had to try. Operation Sunset had begun.

Marcus was stunned. He had been betrayed by the one person he truly trusted and loved. Overriding that stunning betrayal was the fact that he was the instigator for this carnage, and he failed to address it, he should have immediately arrested it instead of prevaricating. He was falling apart, when Freya spoke coldly and firmly: 'Pull yourself together Marcus, there's work to be done. The shield's coming down. You have to help the distributers and organisers now, so people know where to get supplies and what's going on. Our people have put the supplies in situ, and will be giving instructions, but you need to coordinate, remember it's all the old-fashioned way now, no computers, get into the low gear and go or there will be more deaths and anarchy.'

Marcus knew this, he put on hold his intended interrogation of Freya, he'd let those emotions pass unrecognised. His overriding task was to help the organisers restore order in accordance with phase 2 of Operation Sunset, and quickly.

He was in fact, surprised by the efficiency of phase two when he arrived at a previously arranged meeting point. There were of course millions in the movement, all well prepared. They all assisted those not privy to it, directing them to food, shelter and medicinal supplies, along with the basics such as torches, technologically advanced sunshades, pens, paper wind-up clocks, compasses, maps, matches and general survival packages, including full instructions.

CHAPTER 11

The Sunset

The shield had finally disintegrated. There was light. People were terrified and ecstatic at the same time. Out of darkness, there came light. It was biblical. Some primaeval force of nature flowed through the population, making them all feel connected with the natural world and each other. The dark shroud under which they had been living had been replaced by this awesome life-giving wonder, the living world had been touched and warmed and woken. There was a surreal and universal atmosphere of connectivity, of infinite atoms differently formulated into different beings. This manifested in a most incredible cooperation.

The makeshift supply stations were fully operational in all locations. People would gather around their respective station. Notices were displayed, echoing the verbal instructions from the organisers and their people:

'There are more than sufficient supplies for everyone, and they will be fairly distributed. Please be patient.

This is a temporary measure. Further notifications will be given explaining how we will all pull together within separate locations to form a cooperative, growing our food naturally. Our bioengineers have vast stocks of seedlings and protein-based plants along with high nutrient soil.

The digital world is over. This is the beginning of a carbon neutral world. There is now no avenue for over consumption. This is the beginning of the end of global warming.

Please welcome and help our overseas evacuees, some of whom do not speak our language. They have suffered far longer than us, and their lands have been reduced to deserts, or flooded, as a result of our overconsumption. They will remain uninhabitable because of the early lowering of the shield.

Regrettably, there has been a terrible loss of life in getting to this point. In mitigation, that loss does not exceed the previous loss of life during the time of the shield, the fallout from mental illness and poor physical health was equally catastrophic.

If we all cooperate and help one another we will all survive.

Signed

The Dawnbreakers.

June 2075

Folks were busying about, digging, sewing, mending, creating. They sang and danced. In each location there was a flourishing cooperative.

Sadly, the utopia was short lived. Medical supplies were running out, and there was no infrastructure capable of accommodating further manufacture. Regular fights would break out over the shortness of supply.

Gustav Watson was determined to get antibiotics for his sick mother Hilda. If Gustav wanted something, he would get it. It didn't matter who he trod on or manipulated, ultimately, he would succeed.

It was amazing that Hilda had survived thus far, she was just shy of 90 years old to Gustav's 40 years. He was the product of artificial insemination from frozen eggs, in the days when fertility was a choice at any age. Hilda was, in her day, a totally modern woman and embraced advances in fertility, giving her career opportunities she never would have had. She greatly resented criticism of her life choices, whose business was it anyway? Only her beloved husband Frank totally supported her choices, but he died of a brain tumour shortly before Gustav was born, though he was, in fairness, 20 years Hilda's senior. That was probably why Gustav became Hilda's 'project' and later, in her eyes he was the maestro, could do no wrong, and should have whatever he wanted.

Gustav hatched a plan, which involved recruiting several like-minded people. The object was to devise a way to steal the remaining antibiotics for their own families. The rules were that children had first call on medicinal supplies. That would exhaust them, and his mother wouldn't survive without a large dose of broad-spectrum antibiotics.

'Jenny, how's your Dad?' Gustav enquired. Jenny had taken a liking to him and was often 'following' him, Gustav had decided he could turn this intrusion to his advantage.

'He's very poorly, the wound is looking like gangrene is setting in, and he's not by any means in the first blush of youth.' Gustav approached several in like circumstances to himself and Jenny: He assessed them, rejected some and used his manipulative techniques on the chosen few.

Different locations all had their own protective measures regarding supplies, depending on the nature of each co-operative. Some were almost working as one, while others were considerably more individualistic. At Gustav's location, 'compound 666' there was just a nod to protection. Norman, an Old English Sheepdog, 11 years come September, had his kennels outside. Most of his days were spent, like his nights, asleep. The noise from the shield coming down had scuppered his already dodgy hearing, but still, not completely. His sense of smell, however, was next to none. He could tell those he liked or disliked from far afield. He loved his guard dog life and was rewarded with immense love and affection and a good supply of tasty morsels.

Gustav and his newly acquired gang were brazen enough to completely ignore Norman as being any threat whatsoever. 'Not worried about that old hearthrug, not worth the effort of trying to poison him, he's half dead anyway, sleeps all hours, deaf, can't see with all that hair,' Gustav chuckled. He hated dogs, and indeed all animals, he was not too keen on humans either.

'We wait until midnight, and help ourselves, don't really need a lookout, but Joe will fill the role anyway. Fernandez and I will do the grab. Melanie and Terence will be ready with a decoy in case anyone is around. We don't need to

fret over fingerprints or any of that rubbish; so, sorted.'
The accomplices nodded to Gustav in agreement.

There was silence at midnight, Fernandez and Gustav grabbed
the medicines and walked out, taking a shameless shortcut
past Norman's kennel. Norman's nose twitched, if his ears
could prick up, they would have done. He caught the smell
of Gustav in the air. The OES was bred to guard sheep, and
if necessary fight a wolf, having a jaw superior to many a
wild beast, it was just camouflaged under a voluminous
mass of fur.

'Shit, run,' cried Fernandez to his fellow thieves, as he witnessed Norman's teeth sinking into Gustav's jugular. 'We
have to help him,' cried Joe and then promptly fled with the
others, between Norman's metamorphosis from a soppy
mountain of fluff to a devilish creature, and the sounds of
people stirring, they felt that martyrdom was not for them.

Several inhabitants from compound 666 progressed from
stirring to full alert and came rushing out to find Gustav
on the floor, clutching a box of broad-spectrum antibiotics. He was bleeding profusely from the jugular, with
Norman still pinning him down, with bright red fresh
blood around his otherwise white furry muzzle. Someone
called Norman off and found no pulse. Gustav was dead.
Hilda survived long enough to learn of her son's demise.

A fresh notification was sent to all compounds, a labo-
rious task given the distances, confirming what people
knew already. 'The cooperatives will dissolve into anarchy
if there is widespread cheating, thieving and violence.'

CHAPTER 12

The end of Civilization

June 2080

A statue of Norman, made of clay, stood in compound 666. It was a monumental deterrent, and no doubt lessened the workload of Florence, Gabriel and Julia. There were three new Old English Sheepdogs, descendants of Norman, who carried out their guard duties with aplomb. It had taken a considerable strategic effort to find Norman a mate in his late years. But he rose to the occasion, and soon Marigold was pregnant, Beatrice, Nola, and Bob, her other pups, were dispatched to other compounds. Marigold stayed with Norman until his end, returning to her own compound to be reunited with her other pups.

Not all compounds however, had such 'civilised' protection. Sadly in some parts tougher measures were called for. But it often went too far. In some parts, 'criminals' were ostracized, which was worse than it sounded. They were dispatched by force from their communities without supplies. They would have to walk miles and miles to the next location, where, assuming they hadn't perished on route, they might or might not be allowed in. It was pure providence whether they stumbled on a 'compassionate' compound, or one controlled by over-zealous vigilantes.

The world had become a piecemeal mass of self-governing cooperatives. Some worked well, others did not. On the positive side, the world was, as far as all could see, returning to some sort of equilibrium. Plants and wildlife flourished, the soil was fertile, and the seasons made sense again.

Much to Freya's great surprise, Marcus had long since forgiven her. He even went so far as to agree that on balance, it had been the right thing to do. Sadly though, not for them. Their 'leadership' had long been rejected in favour of those with less cerebral and more 'hands on' leadership qualities, and they found themselves being ordered about in their compound 607. Planting seeds all day was not really Freya's thing, and Marcus was finding it hard to adjust to a life revolving purely around digging the soil. They never made love any more, he was too tired with the constant physical labouring, and worse maybe, Freya had so switched off, so her active enquiring mind stopped agitating her, that she didn't mind.

'Marcus, come on, put some welly into it will you, or you'll be on smaller rations,' shouted the section 5 land supervisor. Simultaneously Freya was being admonished for her poor-quality seeding.

That night they both returned dejected, bored, burnt out. 'Fuck it,' Marcus suddenly spurted out, 'Why don't we just leave? I know where we can get a boat, a bit of a trek but doable. We could go to that little island off Hampshire.'

'I remember,' Freya replied. 'You said, last time we went there, that when we returned, there would be real stars, real moonlight and a real sun.'

Marcus laughed. 'You bet, and it's not just the words I remember either.' They both laughed until they physically ached.

Sailing across the Solent was enchanting, the sea sparkled like a mass of tiny crystals as the sun threw out its magical rays. They stared, awestruck. 'Hey look, there's Venus!' Marcus spoke with excitement and joy, he hadn't felt this way for many a year, so engrossed they nearly forgot to alter the sails, though it hardly bothered them, they had been skirting the boundary of life and death all their lives. They moored in the southernmost part and found a most beautiful botanical garden with exotic fauna and flora, and huge plants with brightly coloured flowers, they found lizards, red squirrels, owls. The soil appeared unbelievably fertile with fig, apple, pear plum and all manner of trees. Yes, they had sailed into paradise.

June 2090

The years passed. They were blessed with three wonderful children who they loved and nurtured with all their hearts. They created a home, wrote books for their children, and proceeded to educate them well. They adapted to their environment with love, skill, and respect. Days were spent fishing, swimming, playing, writing reading, growing foods, taming wild animals, forming friendships with like-minded people with whom they truly related and found great joy. The children had many friends. 'Daddy, Daddy 'called Adam, 'I've done it on my own now, caught fishes for supper, enough for us all.' Marcus felt a warm rush of overwhelming love and pride. It just couldn't get better, but it did when he saw the beauty and skill in Joshua's painting. 'Mummy, can you give me some more puzzles, and make them a bit more challenging this time?' Freya was delighted that Evelyn was such a brilliant young woman.

Everything was just idyllic …until that day in September.

Marcus and Freya had, in an age-appropriate way, explained to Adam, Joshua and Evelyn, about the history of global warming, the shield, their part in its premature destruction, and life before and after.

September 1st 4pm

'Mummy, Daddy, I am really confused.' Evelyn was agitated. 'I just don't understand, if people could be cured of bad diseases, then my friend Bobby wouldn't have died, would he? And you said you could flick a switch and there would be light, and there were lights outside, so your friend Jules' Daddy wouldn't have fallen off the cliff when he went the wrong way looking for Johnny's kitten, and you said they could reach people all over the world by a machine called a computer, so it wouldn't just be us few people here would it? And you said they had machines that would wash and clean things for you, so we wouldn't have to spend a day washing things in the stream, would we? I can't believe there were things that meant you could cover a distance of miles in seconds. What happened to all those music things you talked about, so you could listen to great composers? We will never see the great wonders of the world you mentioned, because we cannot get there, nor those works of art you went on about, nor all the different, amazing people all over the world, we will never know them. It is pretty here, but it is suffocating, I feel stifled, not free. They lived exciting meaningful lives. By now, the shield would be down, and people would have those lives again, well us children would, or didn't you care about us?'

There was discussion about refusal to adopt carbon quotas. This time Adam had his say: 'Why didn't you force them to take them, make it law, why didn't the people whose lands were flooded or those turned to sand fight back? Why were the rulers letting people be greedy? Why didn't they shoot them? A war and tough laws would be better than what you did, and easier.'

Evelyn piped up: "Mum told us that in WW2 people were fine with having rationing and with having homes and lands requisitioned, because they knew and understood why this was happening. So, why were people not prepared to do the same with carbon rationing?' Marcus rambled on about people being different then with changing values and social mores.

Joshua had painted another picture while they were all talking and thinking. He held it up. They all gasped: it was a painting of Adam and Eve ...and the serpent.

The author

Tanya White was born in London in 1960. After
finishing university, she trained as a barrister and
over a long career has practised in many fields,
most recently human rights and immigration
law. For many years she has worked from home
rather than the more conventional setting of
Chambers in London. Ms White is married and has
three grown-up children and a grandchild and is
grateful to have finally found the time to follow
her dream and write. The Thirty-Year Night is her
first published fiction. As well as being a writer,
she is a keen gardener and conservationist.

The publisher

*He who stops
getting better
stops being good.*

This is the motto of novum publishing, and our focus
is on finding new manuscripts, publishing them and
offering long-term support to the authors.
Our publishing house was founded in 1997, and since
then it has become THE expert for new authors and
has won numerous awards.

**Our editorial team will peruse each manuscript
within a few weeks free of charge and without
obligation.**

You will find more information about
novum publishing and our books on the internet:

w w w . n o v u m - p u b l i s h i n g . c o . u k